Danny Dunn and the Homework Machine

DANNY DUNN
and the
Homework Machine

by Jay Williams & Raymond Abrashkin

Illustrated by Ezra Jack Keats

McGRAW-HILL BOOK COMPANY

NEW YORK   TORONTO   LONDON

Also by Jay Williams and Raymond Abrashkin

DANNY DUNN AND THE ANTI-GRAVITY PAINT
DANNY DUNN AND THE AUTOMATIC HOUSE
DANNY DUNN AND THE FOSSIL CAVE
DANNY DUNN AND THE HEAT RAY
DANNY DUNN, TIME TRAVELER
DANNY DUNN AND THE WEATHER MACHINE
DANNY DUNN ON A DESERT ISLAND
DANNY DUNN ON THE OCEAN FLOOR
DANNY DUNN AND THE VOICE FROM SPACE

Eleventh Printing

Library of Congress Catalog Card Number: 58-10015

This book is for the little Foxes—
Jane and John

The authors are deeply grateful to Miss Terry di Senso, who guided us through two of the giant computers of the International Business Machines Corporation, and to Dr. Louis Robinson, Manager of the Mathematics and Applications Department, IBM, for his assistance, information, and painstaking reading of the manuscript. In all fairness to both Professor Bullfinch and Danny, we wish to point out that their position on homework is supported by Bulletin 1248–3 of the Educational Service Bureau, University of Pennsylvania.

Contents

Contents

CHAPTER ONE

The Face at the Window

Danny Dunn bent over a strange device that hung from the ceiling of his bedroom, directly over his desk. His red hair was tousled, and the thick freckles of his face were scrambled into a frown of concentration. His best friend, Joe Pearson, a thin, sad-looking boy, stood nearby with his hands deep in his pockets.

"Think it'll work?" Joe asked.

The apparatus consisted of a flat piece of wood about eighteen inches long. A ball-point pen was fixed into each end of it, at a slight angle. The bar of wood was supported by two pieces of clothesline which ran up to pulleys fastened to the ceiling, and then through a double pulley on one wall. A counterweight was fastened to the ends of the line. Beneath each pen was a sheet of paper.

"We'll see," said Danny. "I'll try the first example."

He pressed down on the center of the bar, and

11

"It looks like my invention is a success."

began moving it slowly. Both pens began to write at the same time:

"746 × \$.24 = \$179.04."

"Wow!" Joe cried. "You did it! Two at once."

Danny straightened with a grin. "Yep, it looks like my invention is a success. We can do two homeworks in the time it takes to do one."

Joe rubbed his nose thoughtfully. "I just thought of something. Won't Miss Arnold catch on? They both look alike."

"I thought of that, too," Danny replied. "But we can fix it. By putting the papers at slightly different angles, we can make the handwriting look different. Now I can do our arithmetic homework while you're doing our English homework. It'll save us about half an hour for baseball practice."

He studied the writing for a moment and then sighed. "If only we could save even more time. You'd think six hours of school would be enough for them, without making us take school home. If only I could build some kind of a robot to do all our homework for us. . . ."

"Now, wait a minute," Joe said hastily. "Let's not go overboard. I'm still not sure there won't

13

be some kind of trouble from this pen board, like there generally is when you start inventing things. So far, I'll admit, it looks all right. But if you built a robot, we'd be in trouble for real."

"Gee, thanks," Danny said sarcastically. "Do you really think I could build a robot like that? Don't be crazy. Come on, let's rig the second pen board and you can start on the English home-work."

"Okay," said Joe. "Got some more rope?"

Danny shook his head. "I already used some of my mother's clothesline. I don't dare swipe

any more. You'll have to get a piece of your own."

"All right. I'll run home. I'll be back in ten minutes."

Joe started for the door. "Lucky it isn't Monday," he added. "She hasn't got any wash out today."

As soon as Joe had left, Danny began fastening two more pens into slanted holes he had drilled in another piece of wood. He was working away, completely absorbed, when a noise attracted his attention.

He glanced up with a puzzled frown. There it was again—a kind of tapping. It seemed to come from the window. He put down the board and went to the little alcove in which he had his short-wave radio. The window was just above the radio table.

Next moment, he had frozen in his tracks. His eyes opened wide, and his jaw slowly dropped.

His bedroom was on the second floor of the house. But a face was peering in at him, as if suspended in mid-air.

For a second, Danny couldn't believe his eyes. The face was that of a girl. She had a turned-up nose, wide blue eyes, and shining brown hair gathered into a pony tail. Her lips moved, but Danny couldn't hear her speak. Then she pointed upwards.

"She's trying to tell me where she came from!" Danny said to himself. "My gosh! The moon!"

He pushed the radio table aside, and threw open the window.

CHAPTER TWO

The New Girl

"Hello," said the face.

Danny stared. "You—you can speak English?"

"Sure. Why not?"

"But-but-but I thought—"

"What?"

"Well—how'd you get out there? What's holding you up?"

"A ladder."

Danny stuck his head out the window. "Oh," he said, in disappointment. "I see."

"My name's Irene Miller," the girl said. "My father is Dr. Miller, the astronomer. He's going to teach at Midston University, here in town. We just moved in next door."

"Oh yes. Professor Bullfinch was talking about it. He said Dr. Miller was moving in last night, but I didn't know he—well, I didn't know there was a girl in the family."

"Well, there is. I'm sorry to bother you like

17

this," Irene went on, "but my balloon is on your roof."

"Your balloon?" Danny could not help smiling. "You look kind of old to be playing with balloons."

"I know what you mean," the girl laughed. "But this is a weather balloon. I sent up an anemometer on it."

"To measure the wind speed?"

"Yes. I wanted to see if the wind velocity was high enough so I could do some kite flying."

Danny looked at her with awakening interest, and a certain amount of respect. "Hey!" he said. "That's not a bad idea."

"Glad you like it. Well, the balloon is stuck on your roof, and I thought I could climb up and get it, but the ladder isn't long enough."

"I'll get it for you," Danny said. "Come on in. I'll be right back."

He went out into the hall and climbed the stairs to the attic. A small dormer window let him out on the roof. The balloon, a plastic one with the wind gauge fastened to the line below it, was caught on the television antenna. Danny cut it free, opened the valve to deflate it, and carried it into the house with him.

Back in his bedroom, he found Irene examining the pen board.

"I'll bet you don't know what *that* is," he said, tossing the balloon on a chair.

"No. Some kind of writing machine?"

"Sort of. It's an invention of mine, so one person can do two homework papers at the same time."

Irene looked doubtful. "It—it doesn't seem exactly honest to me," she said.

"Why not?" Danny demanded. "What's wrong with it?"

"Well, for the other person—it would be like copying somebody else's homework, wouldn't it?"

Danny blushed. "Not if they really know how to do the work anyway. And Professor Bullfinch says that homework doesn't have much to do with how a kid learns things in school."

"Professor Bullfinch?"

"Professor Euclid Bullfinch. He knows about most things. He's a physicist, and an inventor—like me," Danny said proudly. "This is his house. I live with him."

"All alone? Which of you does the cooking?"

"Huh? No—I mean, my mother and I live

19

with him. My father died when I was just a baby. My mother took the job of being Professor Bullfinch's housekeeper. The Professor's my—my best grown-up friend. He's a great man. He has taught me everything he knows."

"Goodness! That must be an awful lot to remember."

Danny glanced sharply at her to see if she was making fun of him, but her face was perfectly innocent.

"Well, believe me," he said, "what Professor Bullfinch doesn't know isn't worth knowing. He has his own private laboratory, and he's invented all sorts of things. He has done experiments with gravity, with nuclear particles, with guided missiles—he even improved on HIG. . . . Oh, but you wouldn't know what that is," Danny added loftily.

"No? Why wouldn't I?" Irene asked.

"Well, because . . . I mean—"

"HIG is the abbreviation for a hermetically sealed integrating gyroscope, used in inertial navigation of aircraft," Irene said, with just a suspicion of a smile. "Want me to go on?"

Danny's mouth hung open, but for a second or two no sound came out. Then he said, "How—?"

20

"—did a mere girl come to know such a thing? Is that what you were going to say?"

"Uh—no. No, no. I was just going to say, 'How interesting.' "

"Yes, it is rather interesting. Particularly in the way the axis of the gyroscope in HIG is used to make corrections in the direction of a—"

"No, I didn't mean that," Danny interrupted. "I meant that it's interesting that you know about science."

"Why not? Didn't you ever hear of women scientists, like Madame Curie, the discoverer of radium?"

"Oh, well—sure!"

"I'm going to study physics when I get to college," Irene continued, calmly. "Speaking of HIG . . . of course, you are familiar with the principle of the Schuler-tuned pendulum?"

Danny swallowed, and ran his fingers desperately through his hair. He looked frantically around him. Then, fortunately for him, there was a step on the landing and the bedroom door opened. It was Joe.

"Hi, Joe," Danny called with relief. "Come in. I want you to meet somebody."

Joe stared. "Why, it's a girl!" he said.

"What's the matter? Haven't you ever seen

21

Joe stared. "Why, it's a girl!" he said.

one this close before?" Irene asked, a little put out at his tone.

"No. I mean, sure I have. But where'd you come from?" Joe said.

"This is Irene Miller," Danny said quickly. "She lives next door. They've just moved in."

"Hello," Joe said gloomily. "I hope you'll be happy living around here. But I doubt it. It's a terrible neighborhood."

Irene laughed. "Oh, I don't know. It doesn't seem so awful. The natives are friendly enough, when they aren't trying to impress people."

Danny grinned. "I'm not so bad when you get to know me. I really have a heart of gold. I'm sorry I sounded snooty."

"Want me to play soft music for you both, like in the movies?" Joe put in, sourly. "Let's get back to work, Dan."

"Mmhm. Irene doesn't think my invention is honest."

Joe looked disgusted. "What did you expect from a girl?" he said. "She wouldn't say that if she knew the kind of homework we have to do."

"What kind do you have to do?" Irene asked.

"Well," Danny answered, "for tomorrow, for instance, we have to read fifteen pages of the social studies book and write a short essay on some

South American seaport, and—let's see—oh, yes, answer all parts of eight questions at the end of the chapter."

"Whee-ew!" Irene gave a low whistle. "That seems like an awful lot for just one subject."

Joe said, with a kind of mournful pride, "You see? I told you this was a terrible neighborhood."

Danny put in, "Miss Arnold has always been a good teacher. Only in the last term she's begun to pile up the homework on us. Some idea of hers, to get us ready for high school. Aside from that she's really okay."

"Oh, she's all right," Joe growled. "But I wish we had a man teacher. Women are nothing but trouble."

Irene bristled. "Oh, is that so?"

"Now wait a minute, Joe," Danny said, quickly. "You've got to admit there are plenty of good women in the world. Like—like Madame Curie, for instance. And you shouldn't say things like that anyway. Think of Irene—"

"I didn't mean Irene. She's not a woman anyhow, she's a girl."

"But she knows more about science than most guys do," Danny went on. "She even knows HIG."

24

"Hig who?" asked Joe.

"Not Hig who. It's not a person."

"No? What is it?"

"It's a—er—a hermetically sealed integrating gyroscope."

"Ah! Why didn't you say so in the first place?" said Joe. Then he thought for a minute. "So she knows Hig," he said. "Is that good?"

Before Danny could answer, his mother called from the stairs, "Danny!"

Dan went out into the hall. Mrs. Dunn, a red-haired woman with a merry face, was standing at the foot of the stairs.

"Yes, Mom?" Danny said.

"Why don't you come down and have a snack, now? Milk and fresh doughnuts."

"Gee, swell! We'll be right down."

"Fresh doughnuts," Joe sighed, joining Danny on the landing. "Now *that's* something I can understand. When I said 'women,' I didn't mean mothers."

"And my mother makes them better than any-one in town," Danny said to Irene. "It was lucky for you that your balloon got stuck on the roof, after all."

"Oh, it wasn't pure luck," Irene remarked, with a sly smile. "I did it on purpose."

25

Danny gaped at her. "What?"

"You see, my mother talked to your mother this morning, and I found out all about you. I thought it would be a good way to get to meet you. I think a scientist should leave as little as possible to chance . . . don't you?"

Speechless, Danny nodded.

And Joe, following them down the stairs, shook his head and muttered to himself, "I take it back again. Women! Nothing but trouble."

CHAPTER THREE

Snitcher

In the week that followed, Irene found that Danny's judgment about the school had been correct. There was a good deal of homework, but Miss Arnold was a good teacher. She liked the boys and girls she taught, and she had many exciting ideas that made the classroom work fun. Irene quickly made several friends and became quite popular. The only thing that disturbed her was the way Eddie Philips, who sat in the row on her left, kept staring at her.

Eddie was a stocky, broad-shouldered boy with a heavy face and thin, blond hair. From the time Irene first took her seat, Eddie stared at her, and this made her so nervous that for a day or two she could not pay full attention to the teacher.

On Friday, during the science period, he was staring at her when Miss Arnold called on him to answer a quite simple question. Eddie got up and stammered foolishly, and it was only the bell that saved him. After school, as Irene was starting for home, he came up to her.

"Hello," he said. "Can I—can I carry your books for you?"

"No, thank you," said Irene. "I'm perfectly capable of carrying my own books."

"Oh. Well, can I walk you home?"

"I can't stop you from walking in any direction you like," Irene tightened her lips, and then added, "Just as I can't stop you from staring at me so much in school."

"I wasn't staring. Just looking hard."

"Try looking soft, then. And mind your own business, and maybe you'll be able to answer Miss Arnold's questions."

Eddie flushed. "Aw, I know that science stuff cold."

"Really? You didn't seem to know it today."

"That's because I was thinking of—of somebody."

Just then Danny and Joe came up. Danny said, "Hi, Irene. Let me take your books."

"Oh, thank you, Danny," Irene said primly, handing them to him.

"What are you looking at, Snitcher?" Danny said to Eddie. "See something funny?"

"Yeah. Very funny," said Eddie, staring belligerently at Danny. Scowling, he turned away. "And maybe I'll have the last laugh," he added, over his shoulder, and left them.

"Why did you call him 'Snitcher'?" Irene asked, as they began walking.

"Because that's what he is," Danny replied. "He's always telling on kids—not so much be-

cause he wants to get something for himself. Just out of meanness."

"Well, whatever he is, I wish he'd stop staring at me in class. He makes me nervous."

Joe was walking on Irene's other side, gloomily muttering to himself. He stopped long enough to say, "He thinks you're pretty. *Ha!*"

"Oh, so that's what it was." Irene could not help smiling.

Danny saw her smile. "Gosh, don't tell me you like him," he said. "That creep!"

"I can like anyone I want to," Irene retorted. "I like all sorts of people—I even like Joe."

Joe blinked at this. Irene paid no attention to him, but went on, tossing her pony-tail, "So there, Danny Dunn."

Danny began to look a little hurt. She peered at him with such a merry grin, however, that he cheered up at once.

"Come on over to my house," he said. "Mom made some ginger cookies this morning."

But when they entered the pleasant house of Professor Bullfinch, all thoughts of cookies were at once forgotten, for the place looked as though a miniature tornado had struck it. Clothing was strewn about the living-room floor, papers and notebooks covered the dining-room table, and a trail of odds and ends littered the staircase. As they looked in astonishment, Professor Bullfinch came bustling from the laboratory. He was a short, plump man with a round bald head. He wore thick-framed glasses, behind which his calm eyes twinkled. At the moment, his forehead was wrinkled and he looked disturbed.

"I know I put it somewhere!" he exclaimed. "Danny, my boy. Where on earth is my pipe?"

"You're holding it in your hand, Professor."

"I am? Why, so I am. Thank you, Dan. I knew I could depend on you."

Mrs. Dunn came into the hall with an armful of clothes. "Hello, kids," she said. "The cookies are on the kitchen table. Mr. Bullfinch, here are your shirts, all ironed. For goodness' sake, now, don't throw them into your suitcase carelessly. You aren't usually so absent-minded. Just don't get excited."

"No, Mrs. Dunn. I won't."

"I'm going to put your papers in the briefcase."

"Thank you, thank you, Mrs. Dunn." The Professor mopped his face thoughtlessly with one of the clean shirts. "I'll try to sort them out on the train."

"Oh, dear," sighed Mrs. Dunn. "Look at those stairs."

"Eh? What's wrong with them?"

"There's nothing wrong with the stairs—except that no one can get past your toothbrush and your comb and your razor and these socks. . . . Will we ever get you together?"

"What's happening?" Danny asked. "Where are you going?"

"To Washington," answered the Professor. "I just received a wire from my old friend, Dr. Grimes. He has arranged a series of meetings which he wants me to attend with the representatives of several national bureaus. We are going to discuss work on a nonstop, round-the-world weather rocket, with particular attention to using my new computer.

"And that reminds me," he added. "I want you to come into the lab with me, Dan. There's something very important I have to tell you."

CHAPTER FOUR

Meet Miniac

Professor Bullfinch's laboratory was a long, low structure at the rear of the house, reached by a short hallway. It was crowded and cluttered with equipment, but at one end a large space was clear. Here, there was a curved desk on which were a typewriter and a microphone. A high panel at the back of the desk was filled with tiny light bulbs. There were a number of flat, square buttons, each with a colored panel above it. And beyond the desk was an oblong, gray metal cabinet, about the size of a large sideboard, with heavy electric cables leading to it.

"Danny," said the Professor gravely, dropping his shirts on a chair, "I have decided to give you a big job. I'm sure you can do it. I'm going to leave Miniac in your care."

"What?" cried Joe. "You're going to leave a maniac in his care? He's not old enough."

"*Miniac*, Joe," Danny said. "It's the Professor's new computer." He pointed to the desk and cabinet. "The first midget giant brain."

Professor Bullfinch blinked, mildly. "*Midget* giant?" he said. "That's a little confusing, Dan. Let's just say it's the world's smallest automatic computer."

"And you call it Miniac?" Irene asked, with interest.

"Short for 'miniature automatic computer,'" Danny explained. "Gosh! it's exciting. The Professor finished work on it yesterday. You know, scientists have been trying to make these electronic brains smaller. The Professor has invented a new type of tiny switch and a narrower magnetic tape. Those made it possible for him to build a computer as small as this."

"It doesn't look so small," Joe remarked.

"Dr. Aiken's Mark I computer, at Harvard, the first of the so-called giant brains, filled a whole room," said the Professor.

Joe was eyeing the machine in fascination. "So that's one of those mechanical brains," he said. "Is it thinking now?"

"No, Joe," said the Professor. "It only thinks when we ask it questions."

"You mean you can *talk* to it?"

"Yes, that is one of my improvements. You speak into the microphone, there on the desk, and it types its answers on this electric type-writer."

"Kind of spooky, isn't it?" said Joe, in awe. "I wonder what would happen if you sang into the microphone? Would it type do-re-mi?"

"That's a very interesting idea," said the Professor. "Perhaps we'll try it when I get home. Meantime—uh—you can be rehearsing."

"Professor," Irene said shyly, "could we—could we ask it a question? Just to see how it works?"

Professor Bullfinch stroked his chin. "I don't see why not. Of course, Danny knows its general operation—he has seen me working on it for more than a year."

"Go ahead, Irene," Danny said. "You try. Ask it one of our homework problems."

The Professor snapped a couple of switches. From the cabinet, a steady soft humming came. Several colored lights went on.

"Talk into the microphone, Irene," he said. "Speak slowly and clearly so that Miniac can understand you and translate your words into electrical impulses."

"I understand." Irene stepped close to the desk—or console, as it was called. "It seems

"It seems strange to ask questions of a machine."

strange to ask questions of a machine, doesn't it?" With a slightly nervous quaver in her voice, she said into the microphone, "Um . . . John buys 20 yards of silk for thirty dollars. How much would 918 yards of silk cost him?"

The Professor pressed one of the flat keys. There was a brief pause. Several tiny lights blinked, then a green light flashed on, and the typewriter began to click as if a ghostly hand were striking the keys.

"$1,377.00," it wrote. And after a second or two, it added, "And worth it."

Joe blinked. "Hey! How does the machine know that?"

"Well," said Professor Bullfinch, "the computer has several different sections. There's the communications console, this desk through which the operator can talk to the machine and the machine can answer. Then there's an arithmetic unit that can work out sums, and a unit that can do comparisons and logical problems. And there's a memory unit in which all its information is stored. It has hundreds of tables and facts in its memory banks. Each fact is stored as an electrical pattern on magnetic tape, so altogether they take up very little room. The machine can look into its memory and tell you whether the price is right."

Irene breathed a long sigh. "It's—it's fantastic, like science fiction," she said. "A machine that can work all sorts of problems, give you answers to anything you want to know! It's kind of Superman!"

The Professor shook his head. "No, my dear," he said. "It is only a kind of supertool. Everything in this machine is inside the human head, in the much smaller space of the human brain. Just think of it—all the hundreds of thousands of switches, core memory planes, miles of wire, tubes—all that's in that big case and in this console—are all huge and awkward compared to the delicate, tiny cells of the human brain which is capable of doing as much as, or more than, the best of these machines. It's the human brain which can produce a mechanical brain like this one.

"The computer can reason," he went on. "It can do sums and give information and draw logical conclusions, but it can't create anything. It could give you all the words that rhyme with moon, for instance, but it couldn't put them together into a poem."

"Ha! I feel better," Joe said. "People still have something the machine hasn't got."

"That's right. It's a wonderful, complex tool, but it has no *mind*. It doesn't know it exists."

Danny had been bending over the console, peering at it. Now he said, "Look, Professor! The red light is on. That means something's wrong, doesn't it? I'll turn off the power—"

He reached for the switch marked POWER OFF. Before he could touch it, the Professor caught his hand. "Danny," he said, "there you go again, jumping to conclusions. You must not be so headstrong. Now, think again."

Danny blushed. "Oh, yes," he said. "Now I remember. That red light means the typewriter has finished writing. It's the other, larger red light at the top that means electrical trouble."

"Exactly. Remember, my boy—*a scientist takes nothing for granted.*"

"I will remember. I'm sorry, Professor. I was just excited—like you were a while ago. I wasn't thinking."

Professor Bullfinch rested his hands on the boy's shoulders. "I trust you, Dan," he said. "But you must not forget that this is not a toy. It's an electronic brain, a complicated instrument."

Danny nodded. "What do you want me to do?" he asked humbly.

"You can finish feeding all these tables and

data into it. I'll leave the material right here on the console. You can service the machine every morning; you know how to do that. And if you come across interesting material in the weekly *Science News Letter,* or *Scientific American,* you can feed it into the machine. You have the code tables—"

"Yes, Professor."

Irene put in, "Professor Bullfinch, I'm very interested in science. You know, my father, Dr. Miller, has taught me a great deal. Do you think perhaps I could—well, help Danny, once in a while, if he doesn't mind?"

"I don't mind," Danny said.

"Of course you can, my dear." Professor Bullfinch smiled at the girl. "You may be a good influence on him." Then he turned to Danny and put an arm around the boy. "I know you'll be careful."

"I will, Professor. Honest."

"But—hum!—I know you have a habit of jumping right into things and thinking about them afterward. I want you to promise me one thing, and one thing only, Dan."

"Sure, Professor. What is it?"

"I don't think I can change you into a person who is less headstrong. But I want you to promise me that whenever you get one of your sudden, exciting, and interesting ideas for an experiment—"

"Yes?"

"I want you to count up to a million by thousands."

"Gosh!" said Joe. "That'll take him an hour."

"Yes, I know. That's just it," said the Professor. "Well, Danny?"

"Okay, Professor Bullfinch," said Danny soberly. "I promise."

CHAPTER FIVE

The Homework Machine
Is Born

Irene's father, Dr. Alvin Miller, angrily twisted the dial of his television set.

"Drat this blasted thing!" he exclaimed. "This is the fourth day in a row the picture has begun to skip, right in the middle of a program I wanted to see."

Mrs. Miller, a small, cheerful-looking woman with round blue eyes, and brown hair just like Irene's, said gently, "Perhaps it's interference from somewhere in the neighborhood."

"I've checked every house around," Dr. Miller snapped. "I thought of Professor Bullfinch's laboratory at once, but the Professor has been away for the past three days. And there's nothing there except his computer, which wouldn't disturb the TV anyway."

"Well, then," said Mrs. Miller, reasonably, "why don't you just fix it, instead of complaining?"

"I can't. I don't know how to."

"I don't understand it," said his wife. "You can handle all the parts of one of those enormous telescopes of yours, but you can't fix a TV set."

"It's hardly the same thing, for heaven's sake!"

"Please, dear."

"I'm sorry."

"Just—fiddle with the dials or something, dear, the way you do in the Observatory, and maybe it will clear up." And Mrs. Miller, who, like every wife and mother, could do at least three different things at the same time, went back to reading her book and sewing buttons on a shirt.

The cause of the trouble was closer than they thought. Upstairs, in her bedroom, Irene bent over her short-wave radio, completely unaware that she was interrupting her father's television program with her amateur broadcast.

"W9TGM," she said. "W9TGM. This is W9XAG. Come in."

She snapped a switch, and Danny's voice crackled in her earphones. "W9XAG. This is W9TGM."

"Hi, Danny."

"H'lo, Irene. What's up?"

"I've been having some trouble with that grammar homework. Can you help me?"

"Sure, Irene. Wait just a minute."

She could hear an odd crunching noise and Danny saying, "Shut up a minute." Then he said, "Go ahead. What's the question?"

"What's a predicate noun?"

"Huh? A what?"

"A predicate noun. What is it?"

"I can't get what you're saying. Joe's eating an apple. And there's some interference."

"What did you say?"

"I said, Joe's eating an apple. He's chewing awfully loudly."

Irene took off her earphones in exasperation. She went to the bedroom window and opened it. Leaning out, she yelled across the driveway, "Danny! I said, WHAT'S A PREDICATE NOUN?"

Dan stuck his head out his own bedroom window and said, "I'm not deaf. You don't have to yell."

"Well, what *is* a predicate noun?"

"Hmm. Well, a predicate noun is—it's sort of a noun like a preposition. No, I guess it's more like a—well, a—" He rubbed his nose thoughtfully. "I guess I don't know *what* it is," he confessed, at last.

"Oh, gosh. Maybe Joe knows. Ask him."

Danny popped inside, and reappeared in a moment with a disgusted look. "He says a predicate noun is a noun from Predicate, North Carolina."

Then, suddenly, he snapped his fingers. "Hey! I've got a good idea," he called. "Come on over. We'll ask Minny."

"Minny? Who's Minny—your mother?"

"Miniac. The computer."

"Oh, that's right. It would know, wouldn't it?"

She snapped off her short-wave set (but by this time her father had given up trying to get his program and was deep in the pages of a science-fiction magazine) and ran next door to Danny's house.

Danny and Joe met her and ushered her in through the laboratory door. Dan snapped on the lights and went to the silent machine. He turned on the power, waited until the READY light went on, indicating that the machine was warmed up, and then pressed a key that cleared the memory banks and prepared the computer for action.

"All set," he said. "Now, let's see. We first have to figure out exactly how to ask the question so we'll get the right answer. And then we have to give the machine the address of the information."

"The address? You mean where it lives?" Joe asked.

"Yes, in a way. We have to tell it just where to look in its memory for the information we want. The address is a number in code for one of the 50,000 pieces of information the machine can hold at any one time."

Joe gave a long whistle. Danny thought for a moment and consulted a list of figures. Then, turning to the microphone, he said, "This a question on English grammar. 11875. Give me the definition of the grammatical term, 'A predicate noun,' with one example. Reply by typing out (1) definition, and (2) example."

He then pushed a blue key labeled START.

There was a humming sound. Sparks of light winked along the front panel of the console. A green light flashed, and the typewriter clattered to life.

It wrote: "Predicate noun: (1) The noun or nouns in a sentence which express what is said of the subject of the sentence. (2) You are a *fool*."

"Hey!" spluttered Joe. "Watch your language."

"It's not talking to you, Joe," Irene giggled. "That was just the example."

"Hmf! Well, I wish it would choose better examples."

46

Danny pulled the paper from the typewriter. "Okay, Irene," he said. "There's the answer to your problem."

Irene took the paper, while Danny snapped down several switches. He was just about to turn the power off, when suddenly he stopped, frozen, his hand in mid-air.

"Wait a minute," he said, half to himself.

Irene looked at him. She had known Dan for only a short time, but she was already familiar with the wild light that shone in his eyes, and the strange, thoughtful grin that spread over his freckled face whenever he had a new idea.

"Danny!" she said warningly.

"Mm?"

"You've got one of your crazy ideas, haven't you?"

"Well . . . it's not *so* crazy."

"Oh, help," said Joe. "The last time he said that, we built an automobile out of a power lawn mower."

"It worked, didn't it?" said Danny.

"Sure. And we wrecked Mrs. Hanson's flower beds, and busted Jimmy Nelson's bike, and I almost got concussion—"

"Well, this is nothing like that," Danny said.

Irene said firmly, "Danny. You promised Professor Bullfinch that before you jumped into anything you'd count to a million by thousands."

"Oh, yes. That's right."

"Start counting, boy," said Joe.

Danny looked stumped for a moment. Then he said, "Okay. If you're both going to pick on me, I'll do it." And with a sly smile, he added, "Counting to a million that way is the same as adding a thousand each time. And multiplying is just adding a number to itself a certain number of times. Right? Okay, so I'll count to a million by thousands by multiplying. One thousand times itself equals one million. There. I counted to a million by thousands."

Irene frowned. "I *think*," she said, "that that isn't exactly what the Professor had in mind."

Danny beckoned to her and Joe. "Listen," he said, lowering his voice. "Never mind that. This is a really great idea. Why can't we use Minny as a *homework machine?*"

"What?" Irene cried.

"A homework machine?" said Joe. "What's that?"

"Simple. Minny can answer problems in grammar like that one we just asked. She can

answer any kind of arithmetic problem. She can give information, like for social studies. I'll bet, if we set her up properly, she could even write simple compositions. Let's use her to do...." He caught himself and glanced at Irene. "I mean, to help us with our homework, the way she just helped you."

Irene's eyebrows slowly rose. She and Joe looked at each other. Then she said to Danny, "Do you think it would work?"

"Why not? We can try it."

"All right. I'm game," Irene whispered.

"Me too," said Joe, in a whisper. Then he

said, "Hey, Dan. Why are we all whispering?"

Danny glanced round. "I don't want Minny to hear us," he exclaimed. "After all, maybe she hates homework as much as we do!"

CHAPTER SIX

"Who Cares?"

Miss Arnold's class had grown in the past two years, as new families moved into the town and sent their children to school. Dan had heard her tell the principal that she wished she could give more time and attention to each student, but that was no longer possible. There were thirty-seven boys and girls now, where there had once been twenty, and sometimes Miss Arnold couldn't help feeling that there were too many pupils in the world—at any rate, in her part of it.

She said, with a sigh, "So you see, writing five-tenths this way—.5—is just the same as writing it $\frac{5}{10}$. And five-tenths is the same as one-half. Why is that, George?"

George Bessel, a plump, tow-headed boy whose nickname was Fatso, got reluctantly to his feet. At once, two or three girls began giggling, and George glanced angrily at them.

"Uh—" he said.

"Do you know, George?" Miss Arnold asked, gently.

He fidgeted, in despair. "I used to know," he said. "But I guess I forgot."

"Very well. You may sit down."

Sue Parker was waving her hand urgently. She always waved her hand whenever anyone couldn't answer a question.

Before Miss Arnold could call on her, however, a small white object, sailing down one of the aisles just above the floor, caught the teacher's eye. She strode forward and picked it up just as it landed next to Irene Miller's desk. It was a bit of paper, folded into a glider.

"Who threw this?" she demanded.

A dead silence fell upon the class.

Then Eddie Philips said, "Danny Dunn threw it, Miss Arnold. It's a note."

Danny's face was flaming. Ellen Tresselt, who sat behind him, whispered to her neighbor, Victoria Williams, "I know who it was for, too."

"Who doesn't?" Victoria whispered back.

A wave of tittering went through the class.

"A note? Is that true, Dan?" Miss Arnold asked.

Danny nodded. He had banked on Miss Ar-

nold not noticing the little glider because of Sue Parker's waving hand. He thought to himself, "Next time I'll make it out of dark paper, for camouflage." Aloud, he said, "Yes'm."

Miss Arnold crumpled the glider in her hand. "I'm not going to read this, Danny," she said, "and I'm not even going to ask who it was for."

She glanced down at Irene, who was staring studiously at the top of her desk, pretending not to be listening. Like all good teachers, Miss Arnold knew more about her pupils than they thought she did.

"However," she went on, "I must say I'm surprised at you, Danny. School will be over in ten minutes, and anything you have to say to anyone could certainly wait until then. Or, on the other hand, there are the United States mails. I'd prefer not to have my students flying their letters by air mail during class."

She walked back to her desk and turned to face the pupils. "Particularly during a period in which so many of you seem to be doing so poorly," she went on. "Will you all write down the homework assignment for tomorrow, please?"

A groan went through the class. Miss Arnold tightened her lips.

"There's no occasion for all this weeping and wailing, either," she said. "In the first place, you all know that the class has grown a good deal in the last couple of years. That means I can't work with each one of you as much as I used to. It means high school will be overcrowded, too. It also means that there will be more competition for college admissions. It's not easy to get into college these days."

She looked at them and sighed. "I want each of you to have a good chance at the best kind of education," she continued. "People are finding out more and more about the earth—about science, and about each other. That means there's more and more for you to learn. Above all, you have to know how to study these new things. There's no substitute for homework as a way of learning how to study. So I suggest that instead of complaining you all buckle down and *work*."

She flipped open the arithmetic book and said, "You will all do problems one through twenty, on pages 57 and 58."

There was another heartfelt groan from everyone but Danny, Irene, and Joe. Miss Arnold turned to the blackboard and firmly wrote down the assignment.

While her back was turned, Irene glanced at Danny. He winked at her. Soundlessly he shaped the words "Who cares?" with his lips.

He looked over at Joe, who sat two rows away, and did the same thing. Joe nodded and voicelessly said, "Minny."

Eddie Philips, secretly watching the three of them, scowled. He had told Miss Arnold about the glider because he was jealous and hoped to get Dan into trouble. Now, seeing their winks and smiles, he felt anger churning around in him like a stomach-ache.

"I wonder why they're grinning at each other like that," he muttered to George Bessel, who sat in front of him. "You'd almost think they didn't mind all that homework. I'll bet Danny has something up his sleeve."

He narrowed his eyes in suspicion. "Maybe," he added, "just maybe I'll follow him after school and keep an eye on him. I'll get that smart aleck yet. Wait and see."

CHAPTER SEVEN

The Homework Paradise

Danny closed his copy of *The Study of Science* with a sigh, and blinked at Joe and Irene. They were all seated at the console of Miniac, in Professor Bullfinch's laboratory. It was three days later.

"That's the last book," Danny said. "Now Minny knows everything in all our school books."

"Phew!" said Joe, wiping his forehead, "You

know, that was hard work—storing all that information in the machine. I didn't realize there was so much to know. Maybe it'd just be easier to do our homework every day."

"I don't think so," Danny said. "Sure, it was hard work. But now we're free forever."

"Till next term," Irene corrected him.

"Well, that's almost forever. The next step is to program tomorrow's assignment."

He pushed back his chair and got up.

Joe said, "What's all this programming you're always talking about?"

"Wait a sec," Danny said. "I'll just get some refreshments for us. We can use 'em. Irene, you get out tomorrow's homework."

He went down the hall to the kitchen, while Irene arranged their notebooks on the desk and Joe stretched and yawned. Danny returned in a few moments with a plate of chocolate graham crackers and three bottles of Coca-Cola.

Irene said, "The biggest piece of homework we have for tomorrow is twenty problems in arithmetic."

"That's easy," said Danny.

He fed the end of a roll of typewriter paper into the electric typewriter and cleared the memory banks for action.

"Now," he said. "Programming is telling the machine exactly what questions you want answered and how you want them answered. In order to do that right, you have to know just what sequences of operation you want the machine to go through."

"Uh-huh." Joe nodded. "What does that mean?"

"Look. Suppose you want to jump across a ditch—"

"Why?"

"Why what?"

"Why would I want to jump across a ditch."

"Don't be silly. I'm just giving you a for-instance. All right, first you have to figure out how far it is across the ditch. Then you have to look in your memory to see how far you can jump. Then you have to compare the two to see if you can jump this ditch. Those steps are the operations your mind has to go through. The order in which you think of them is their sequence. See?"

"I guess so."

"All right. If we want Minny to give us the right answers to an arithmetic problem, or a history question, we first have to analyze the operations the machine has to go through, and the order in which it does them. Then we put this

59

down on a piece of paper together with the addresses of all the information or the parts of the machine that will be used to solve the problems. That's programming."

"I see." Joe rubbed his nose soberly. "I think I understand that all right. But I still can't figure why I'd want to jump across a ditch. Why couldn't I just walk around it?"

"Oh, forget it," Danny groaned. "Come on. Let's start the problems going."

They first set up and fed into the machine the twenty arithmetic problems. Then the five questions that had to be answered on South American countries. And then the ten problems in English grammar. Danny pressed the START key. Lights began twinkling on the control panel. The machine settled down to a steady humming, and the three friends lolled back in their chairs and ate cookies.

"Gosh!" said Joe, sipping his Coca-Cola. "This is the life!"

"It sure is. We ought to put a sign on the door: 'Happy Homework Hunting Ground,'" said Danny.

Irene peered over at the typewriter, which had just stopped rattling. The red light was on.

"There's your arithmetic, Joe," she said. "Now I guess it'll start on social studies."

"Good old Minny," Joe chuckled. "I'll write a poem in her honor." Joe was known throughout the school for his poems. "You know, we ought to enter her in one of those TV quiz shows. We could make a fortune."

"Um. I somehow have a feeling that Professor Bullfinch wouldn't like that," Danny said, laughing.

"I'll bet he wouldn't," said Irene. "By the way, what are we going to do when he gets home, Dan?"

Danny thoughtfully ate a cookie. "I'll have to ask his permission for us to go on using the machine. But maybe it'll be all right. Anyway," he added, "what's the use of worrying about it now? We may as well enjoy Minny while we have her."

The typewriter, which had been working away industriously, stopped, and the red light went on. "That's the first of the social studies pages," Danny said. "It can be yours, Irene. I'll take the next one, and Joe can take the third."

He pulled out the paper, and at once the typewriter began again.

"It's like magic," Joe said. "A fairy godmother

named Minny, who comes along and gives you a wish. So you wish that all your homework should be done for you. And presto! there it is."

Danny snickered. "When you come right down to it, Joe, it isn't any more magic than a million other things all around us. I mean, in fairy tales the prince is always getting magic sandals that let him fly through the air, or magic eyeglasses that let him look through walls, or a magic servant who can show him what's happening a hundred miles away. . . well, we've got 'em all, nowadays: X rays, airplanes, television—"

"Yes, but this is a different kind of magic. A machine that *thinks*."

"There are thinking machines all over this house—everybody's house," Danny replied. "For instance, refrigerators that know how to keep themselves at the right temperature, and defrost themselves when it's necessary. Or machines that count and add, just like Minny does —the speedometer on your bike, for instance."

"Yes, and ovens that know how to keep themselves hot and turn themselves off when the food's cooked," Irene put in. "Or record players that feel the size of a record, put the needle on in the right place, and stop when the record's over."

"They're all machines that can think in one way or another," said Danny. "Take a thermostat, for instance, like that one."

He pointed to a dial with numbers on it, on the side of the console. Joe reached out to it, saying, "You mean this gadget?"

"Hey, don't touch it!" Danny cried.

"What's the matter? Is it poisonous?"

"Worse than that. The Professor's new switches have to be kept at a certain temperature —98.6°F.—to work properly. As long as that dial is set at that temperature, the machine works. If, for some reason, the inside of the case got too warm, the rising heat would expand a piece of metal inside the thermostat. That would start the refrigerator motor and cool things off. When the temperature was just right, again, the motor would shut off."

Joe inspected the dial. "Gee, what would happen if it didn't work?"

"It's impossible for it not to work," Danny said. "You can tell by looking at it if it's set properly. And I guess good old Minny could tell us if something wasn't right."

"You keep talking about the computer as if it was alive," Irene said. "It's just a machine."

They might not have been so happy if they

had seen the two faces that peeped in at them.

"So's a ship just a machine," said Danny. "But sailors always call their ships 'she.' Minny's so smart that—well, gosh, sometimes I feel she really *is* alive."

The typewriter stopped, then clicked a few times again.

"You see?" Danny said. "She heard me, and she's impatient to get finished."

All three laughed. Danny reached over lazily and pulled the second copy of the social studies homework out of the typewriter.

"Man!" Joe sighed, tipping up his Coca-Cola bottle to get the last drops. "This is the way to do your homework. This is heaven!"

"You said it," Dan agreed. "Does that make us angels?"

They all laughed, but they might not have been so happy if they had seen the two scarcely angelic faces that peeped in at them through one of the laboratory windows that faced a thick clump of lilac.

They were Eddie Philips and George Bessel. Eddie was grinning wickedly. And George, ducking down so he would not be seen, said in a soft voice:

"Boy, wait till Miss Arnold hears about this!"

CHAPTER EIGHT

"Is It Fair?"

At about five o'clock the very next afternoon, the doorbell of the Professor's house rang. Mrs. Dunn, who was in the midst of telephoning a list of parents about a coming Parent-Teachers meeting, looked up in annoyance.

"Danny!" she called. "Will you answer the door, please?"

Danny was performing a very interesting experiment. He was mixing together all the chemicals in his chemistry set that began with "S," just to see what would happen. However he put his important research aside and ran downstairs to open the door.

Miss Arnold stood on the steps. Her lips were pressed tight together, and there was a dangerous look in her eyes.

"Oh, hullo, Miss Arnold," said Danny. "I guess you want to see my mother."

"Yes, Dan, I do."

"About the P.T.A., I suppose?"

"No. About the H.O.M.E.W.O.R.K."

Danny gulped. "Oh," he said, in a very small voice.

He led the way into the living room. His mother, who had recognized Miss Arnold's voice, came out to greet the teacher.

"Why, Miss Arnold," she said. "What a pleasant surprise."

"I'm afraid it's not so pleasant," said Miss Arnold, shaking hands. "I have something serious that I must speak to you about."

"Do sit down." Mrs. Dunn motioned her to a chair. "Danny, why don't you run up to your room—"

"No, I'd rather have him stay. What I have to say concerns him."

"Oh, dear. I hope he hasn't done anything wrong?"

"I'm not sure, Mrs. Dunn." Miss Arnold leaned forward. "I have reason to believe that Danny is letting a machine do his homework for him."

There was a long silence.

Then Mrs. Dunn said, in a worried tone, "Miss Arnold, you've been working too hard."

"What?"

"I've felt it for some time. That class is really

68

too large for one teacher to handle. You ought to take a vacation."

Miss Arnold's mouth fell open.

"I'm going to speak to the Board," Mrs. Dunn went on, but Danny interrupted.

"She's right, Mom. I *have* been using a machine to do my homework."

Mrs. Dunn looked at her son with bewilderment.

"The Professor's computer," Danny explained.

"I don't understand. How can the computer do your homework?"

"Well, first we fed all the information from our school books into it—"

"By 'we' he means Joe Pearson and Irene Miller," Miss Arnold said. "But I know very well that they'd never have thought of it themselves. You know, Mrs. Dunn, I like Danny enormously, and he does very well in school, but you must admit he has a—well, an *active* imagination."

"Yes," said Mrs. Dunn, dryly. "I've known him longer than you have. Go on, Dan."

"Well, then we analyze the problems we have for homework, and we program them, and we let

69

the machine solve them and type them out for us."

"But that isn't fair, Danny," Miss Arnold burst out.

"Why not?" he asked, in surprise.

"Why not? Why, because—well, what would you think of a boy who got his father to do all his homework for him?"

"I'd think he was a pretty smart kid to be able to talk his father into something like that."

"No doubt. But that isn't what I mean. You'd think he wasn't quite honest, and you know it. And he wouldn't be doing himself a bit of good."

"Well," said Danny, slowly, "in a case like that, maybe not."

"I should think not," Miss Arnold said, triumphantly. "You know that that boy wouldn't learn a thing. He'd never get through high school. And he certainly wouldn't have a chance for college. The purpose of homework is to teach you how to study, and to give you a real, sound understanding of the subjects I'm trying to teach you."

"She's right, Dan," Mrs. Dunn said. "Don't you think so?"

70

"Well, sure, Mom. But I *know* these subjects. Gosh, I have to know them so I can program the machine to do them."

"But—then I don't understand. What's the advantage of the machine doing them for you, if you already know them?"

"It's faster. Once we've set them up and fed in the questions, Minny can turn them out in a couple of minutes for all three of us."

"Minny?"

"That's what we call the machine. Short for Miniac."

"I see," said Miss Arnold. "But it still isn't fair—"

"Why not?" Danny protested. "Sure it's fair. Look, I know how to do long division. So why should I spend an hour doing fifty long-division examples, when Minny can do them in a minute? Gee, nobody does arithmetic the long way any more—nobody! Grocers use adding machines, and so do banks. Everybody uses tools to make his work easier. Why, we don't use inkwells and quill pens in school any more, Miss Arnold. We use fountain pens. Those are tools to make our work easier."

"But you can't compare a fountain pen to an electronic brain."

"Sure you can. It's just another kind of tool. Lots of kids do their homework on typewriters. In high school and college they teach kids to do some of their homework on slide rules. And scientists use all kinds of computers as tools for their work. So why pick on us? We're just—just going along with the times."

Miss Arnold said nothing for perhaps a minute. Then she said, slowly, "Danny, I must admit you've got a serious point. I won't force you to stop using the computer. But I'm asking you for your own good not to use it. Children learn through practice. You'll have to take my word for it that it would be better for you to do your homework the old-fashioned way."

Danny set his jaw. "If you want me to be old-fashioned," he said, "I'd better not study modern science. I ought to go back to the old-fashioned idea that the world is flat. I ought to forget about the atomic theory."

"Danny," his mother put in, "please remember that you're talking to your teacher."

He blushed. "I'm sorry, Mom. I *like* Miss Arnold. You know that, and so does she. But I don't see why I have to give up using a perfectly good tool just because I know how to use it and the other kids don't. For instance, would you forbid me to get information out of an encyclopedia, if I had one and the other kids didn't?"

"Hmm . . . No, I suppose not," Mrs. Dunn said, reflectively. "But—"

"Well, the encyclopedia's a tool, too. I use Minny the same way."

Danny turned to his teacher. "I'm sorry, Miss Arnold," he said, in a tone that was respectful but firm. "When you talk about what's fair—I don't think it would be fair to make *us* stop."

Miss Arnold sighed. Mrs. Dunn said, "Very well, Dan. Suppose you go get some coffee for Miss Arnold. I'm sure she'd like some now."

"Yes, I would," the teacher said.

Danny went off to the kitchen. As soon as he was out of the room, Mrs. Dunn drew her chair closer to Miss Arnold's.

"As we were talking," she said, softly, "an idea came to me. I think I know how to solve this problem—and without using a computer, either. Listen, Miss Arnold. . . ."

She began whispering earnestly. And a broad smile slowly spread over Miss Arnold's face.

CHAPTER NINE

Snitcher Confesses

The following morning, which was Saturday, Danny met Joe and Irene and walked with them to a little stream near the campus of Midston University. Here, where an arched iron bridge spanned the stream, the three sat down and dangled their legs over the water, and Danny told of Miss Arnold's visit.

"Doggone it," said Joe, leaning forward to drop a pebble on his own reflection. "I knew it. Dames! Nothing but trouble! Now we'll have to give up using the computer."

"No we won't," said Danny. "She told me she wouldn't force me to stop using it."

Irene thoughtfully polished her nails against her sweater. "Do you think it's right, Dan?" she said.

"Why not?"

"If Miss Arnold thinks it isn't fair—well, maybe it isn't. After all, she is our teacher."

"Of course it's right," Danny said impatiently.

"I told you, she said I had a point. That's the same as saying I won the argument. Forget it. What I'm wondering is, how did she find out about our using the computer?"

"I've got a good suspicion," said Joe. "I'll bet it was Snitcher Philips."

"How could it be? How could he know about the computer?"

"How does he ever know about any of the things he snitches about? Maybe he uses carrier pigeons."

Danny snorted.

"Well, who else could it be?" Joe persisted. "Maybe he followed us home one day and watched us."

"We can find out," said Danny. "Did you ever hear of Mata Hari?"

"Nope. Who was that? Any relative to that guy you once talked about—Hig?"

"No, you dope. Mata Hari was a famous spy, a woman who used to get friendly with soldiers and find out their secrets. I saw her in an old movie on TV."

"Dames—" Joe began.

Irene frowned at him. "Joe Pearson!" she said. "If you say that once more, I'll push you

76

off this bridge into the water. Go on, Danny. What's your plan?"

"*You're* my plan," said Danny. "And Snitcher is the enemy . . ."

Monday afternoon, when class was over, Eddie Philips was just leaving school when, to his astonishment, Irene stopped him.

"Hello, Eddie," she said, in a voice that oozed honey.

"H-hello," he said, staring.

"I wondered if you'd like to carry my books today?"

"Well, gee . . . sure."

He took them from her, looking a little surprised.

"You aren't going around with Danny Dunn any more?" he asked.

"Oh, *him*." Irene shrugged and pouted. "He never talks about anything but his old science stuff. I like a boy who's interested in *lots* of things."

They walked down the street past the drugstore, and Eddie never noticed Joe and Danny peering at him from inside.

Danny glanced up the clock on the wall. "She

77

should just be telling him how smart he is," he remarked.

Joe set his watch. "If we're right, it won't be long now."

Irene and Eddie had turned into Elm Street and were passing the gas station. "I thought the way you answered Miss Arnold's question about Abraham Lincoln was just wonderful," Irene cooed. "You must do an awful lot of studying at home."

"Nah. I don't have to do much. Most of this stuff is pie for me," Eddie boasted.

"Isn't that *wonderful!*" Irene sighed, and fluttered her eyelashes in what she hoped was a Mata Hari manner.

They turned into Maple Street. They were passing the vacant lot where the boys sometimes practiced baseball. Irene stopped walking and looked sweetly at Eddie.

"You know, Danny has been helping me with my homework," she said. "But maybe I'll let you help me, instead, since you know the subjects so well and can do them so easily."

"Swell!" said Eddie. He added, with a grin, "And I won't need any machine, either. I can do it standing on my head."

At the word "machine" Irene, still smiling, reached out and took hold of her books. "Oh, can you?" she said.

There was a wide, deep mud puddle at the edge of the lot. With all her strength she gave Eddie a sharp, sudden push in the chest. He lost his balance and toppled backward with a yell of alarm. He landed square in the middle of the puddle.

"Try standing on your head in *that,* you—you sneak!" Irene snapped.

Danny and Joe, who had been hiding behind an automobile on the other side of the street, stepped out.

"Our timetable worked out fine." Danny chuckled. "That was right on the button."

Then he crossed the street and took Irene's books.

Eddie, spluttering and dripping, glared up from the puddle. "You planned this," he howled at Dan. "She didn't really want me to walk her home, or—or anything!"

"That's right. I planned it," Danny said. "And when Irene pushed you into the puddle we knew you'd given yourself away. So you spied on us and found out about the computer, eh? And

79

She gave Eddie a sharp, sudden push.

He landed square in the middle of the puddle.

you ran to tell Miss Arnold. Well, from now on keep your nose out of our business, see?"

"Yeah," Joe put in. "We're working on an automatic nose nipper."

Eddie was too furious to reply. Irene turned her back on him and walked off between Joe and Danny.

Eddie scrambled out of the puddle with great difficulty. A few moments later, as he was trying to wipe the mud from his face, George Bessel came along with his hands in his pockets.

"Hey, Eddie!" he called. "What you doing? Making mud pies is for little kids."

"Boy! Are you comical," Eddie snarled.

"No kidding, what are you doing?"

"Flying over the Rockies in a balloon." Eddie wrung out his handkerchief and jammed it into his pocket. "Danny Dunn got me into this. That's what happened. But I'll get even with him."

"How?"

"I'll mess up that machine of his so that he'll never do any more homework on it. I'll fix him."

"How can you do that?" George asked.

"I'm not such a dope in science as they think," said Eddie, grimly. "You heard what they were talking about when we were watching them, the other day."

"I heard, but I didn't understand it."

"Well, I understood all right. Just wait, Danny Dunn. Just—you—wait."

CHAPTER TEN

Trouble in Paradise

Miss Arnold was giving the homework assignment. As usual, Danny jotted it down with a smile. But suddenly his heart gave a bump, and he sat up straight in his seat.

"Danny Dunn," Miss Arnold was saying, "and Irene Miller and Joe Pearson. You needn't write down this assignment."

Danny threw a quick glance at Irene. Then he said, "Why not, Miss Arnold?"

"I've got some special work for you three. Come up to my desk right after class. That's all, people. Gather up your things."

The bell rang. As the others trooped out, with many backward looks, the three friends went silently to Miss Arnold's desk. They stood in a row wondering what was coming. Miss Arnold did not keep them long in suspense.

"Well!" she said. "First of all, I must compliment you on your work. You've been doing so well that I'm giving you special homework, for extra credit."

84

Danny gulped. "Sp-special homework?"

"Oh, yes. I'm sure none of you will have any trouble doing it."

She opened her desk drawer and took out half a dozen books. "These are first-year high school algebra and history books. Please do the first five examples in the algebra book, and answer the first eight questions in the history. By tomorrow."

She handed them each two books.

"But—" Danny began.

"And by the way," said Miss Arnold, in a sugary tone, "I want to commend you all for the *neatness* of your *typing,* in your past homework. I do hope you'll keep it up. It makes the work so much easier for me to read."

"But—" said Danny.

"Now, Danny, I know what you're going to say," said Miss Arnold. "You're going to say that you want more to do than just these few problems. Well, we'll see how you make out, and perhaps I'll give you even more homework by next week."

"Ulp!" said Danny.

"Well, that's all, I guess," Miss Arnold said, brightly. "Good-by."

The three plodded gloomily out.

"Fine!" said Joe. "That does it. Oooh, am I sick. I think I'm going to die."

"Oh, stop it," Danny said. "All we've got to do is feed the material from these books into Minny."

"But Dan, it isn't as simple as that," Irene protested. "You know that in order to analyze and program our questions, we have to know how to solve them ourselves."

Joe groaned. "What a happy thought! You're talking to a dead boy. We'll have to study these two books. And by tomorrow!"

"Cut it out," said Danny. "We don't really have to study them. We just have to read them enough to understand what's in them."

Irene looked puzzled. "What's the difference?"

"What do you mean, what's the difference?" Danny said. "The difference is that—well, the difference is— Hm. . . ."

"Oh my poor head," Joe moaned. "I'll never be able to hold all this in it. Women! I told you they were nothing but trouble."

"Joe, you stop that," Irene said, whirling to face him . "Just because Miss Arnold—"

"I'm not talking about Miss Arnold," Joe re-

torted. "If your parents had had a boy instead of a girl, all this would never have happened."

"What are you talking about?" Danny stared at his friend.

"Well, look. If Irene had been a boy, he wouldn't have been good-looking. He'd have been just another ugly kid. And you probably wouldn't have become friends with him. You probably would've had a fight. So you never would have helped him with his homework. So then you never would have had the idea of using the computer. So then we wouldn't be in this jam."

"You're kidding!" Danny said.

"I am, huh? I may be dead, but I'm not kidding. It's her fault. And believe me, I'm through. I'm not going to have anything more to do with her—I'm liable to find myself doing college homework."

"If that's the way you feel," Irene said coldly, "you needn't talk to me again."

Danny looked from one to the other, with real pain. This was the worst sort of complication: his best friends quarreling so bitterly. Somehow, it always seemed that when he jumped into something without thinking of the consequences—as for instance when he had jumped into the idea of using the computer for homework—then all sorts of unforeseen and unhappy things resulted.

"If it's anybody's fault, it's mine," he broke in. "I'm the one who started it. Now, come on. We can't afford to fight, we've got too much to do. Maybe you can stay at my house for dinner, Joe—"

"Oh, I'm sure he doesn't want to work with the computer any more," Irene said. "It would mean he'd have to be in the same room with me."

"I'm stuck with this homework," Joe said, sullenly. "I've *got* to work with the computer."

Danny sighed. "Let's go," he said. "And I wish you two would quit snapping at each other."

Irene turned to him. "You can tell your friend," she said haughtily, "that I'll work with

88

him. But until he learns to be polite, I don't have to talk to him."

The atmosphere in the Professor's laboratory that afternoon was definitely strained as a result of this quarrel. Joe stayed for dinner, and he and Danny didn't have much to say to each other during the meal. Afterward, Irene came back to the lab and they continued with their work, speaking only as much as was necessary.

They had to feed the history and algebra facts into the machine's memory banks, and then give all this material code numbers so that the machine could find it when they asked for it. They had to coach each other on the information contained in the books so that they'd understand the nature of the questions and problems involved, and be able to give Minny the proper instructions when they wanted answers to questions.

They grew sulkier and gloomier and wearier, as it got later. They could not finish both books but had to be content with doing about twenty pages of each. They decided to leave the rest for future sessions. Then they programmed the homework Miss Arnold had given them—the first five examples in algebra and the first eight questions in the history book—and flopped into chairs to rest while Minny ran off three copies of each.

Irene and Joe took their copies.

"So long, Danny," Joe said. "I've got to get home. Tell your friend, Irene, that I said good night."

"Oh, Joe. This is silly," Irene burst out. "Let's make it up. I will if you will."

But Joe was very tired and grumpy. And he was more than a little jealous that Irene had become such a good friend of Danny's.

So he said, "There's nothing to make up about. I still say if you'd never moved in around here, we wouldn't be in this mess."

Irene pressed her lips together. She felt, for a moment, as if she were going to cry. Then she blurted, "You keep talking about how bad girls are. Ha! *You're* nothing but a sorehead. Good night, Danny."

And she stalked out. Joe sighed. He felt that he had been a pig, but it was too late to do anything about it.

"Good night, Dan," he said, softly.

"I'll walk you to the front door," Danny said.

He snapped out the lights in the lab. But he was much too worried about the disagreement between his friends to remember to lock the back

90

door. When he had seen Joe out, he went to the kitchen for a glass of milk.

His mother was sitting at the table with a card file before her, and two or three cookbooks.

"What are you doing, Mom?" he asked.

"I'm programming tomorrow's meals, dear," Mrs. Dunn said, with a twinkle in her eye.

"Oh. Mom—"

"Yes?"

"What do you do when your best friend has a fight with your other best friend?"

Mrs. Dunn thoughtfully chewed the eraser of her pencil. "It seems to me, darling," she said, at last, "that if the middle of a rope is strong, it won't break no matter how much you pull on both ends."

Danny looked at her. "Oh," he said. "I—I think I understand. Well, good night, Mom."

He started up the stairs. Then he remembered that he had forgotten to lock up the laboratory. As he entered, it seemed to him that he heard an odd, scrambling noise out in the lilacs. But when he looked, there was nothing there. He turned the key in the back door, snapped off the lights, and went up to bed.

CHAPTER ELEVEN

A Scrambled Report

Danny overslept the next morning. His mother had to call him three times, and in the end she had to come upstairs and roll him out of bed before he would get up. He came down yawning, and Mrs. Dunn, lifting one eyebrow, said, "You'll have to be more serious on school nights, Dan. No more late game playing with your friends."

"Game playing!" Danny exclaimed. "Oh. Yes, Mom."

He gobbled his breakfast and went out. Irene emerged from her front door at the same time, rubbing her eyes.

"You had trouble getting up, too, I see," she said.

"Uh-huh. I'll bet Joe did, too."

Irene shook her head. "I wish Joe wasn't so stubborn."

"Aw, he was just tired last night. All that new homework got him."

Irene clapped a hand to her mouth. "Oh, my goodness!" she said. "Danny! I forgot."

"Forgot what?"

"When you said 'new homework,' I remembered some *old* homework. Last week Miss Arnold asked me to do a social studies report. I'm supposed to give it in class this morning. And I never prepared it."

"Oh, gosh. I remember it—it was on the products of Peru."

"That's right. We were so busy last night, I forgot all about it."

Danny looked at his wrist watch. "Listen," he said, "you go on to school. All that stuff is in Minny's memory. If I program it right now, I can get it for you in three minutes."

"But will it be in the form of a report?"

"Why not? It's just information we want, and the machine can dig it out of the tapes and type it."

"But Dan, you'll be late for school."

"So what? We'll both be late if you don't hurry. Anyway, maybe I can just make it in time."

Without another word, he turned and dashed back. He rushed into the house, shouted to his mother, "Forgot something!" and ran to the laboratory. He snapped the POWER ON switch and, while he was waiting for the machine to warm

He ducked under a line of fluttering wash.

up, quickly jotted down exactly what he wanted and found the code number for its place in the memory banks. Turning to the microphone, he said, "Address 21690. A report on the products and industry of Peru. Prepare and type information, pages 93, 94, and 95."

He tapped the proper key, and within a moment or two the typewriter was rattling off the report. Danny snatched it out of the machine, switched off the power, and ran.

He knew a few short cuts which he usually didn't like to use because they meant going through the back yards of some rather grumpy people, but this morning he couldn't stop to worry about that. He climbed a couple of fences, ducked under a line of fluttering wash, crossed a little bridge, ran uphill through a birch wood, and came out at the edge of the athletic field. He made it to the classroom just as the first bell rang, dropped the paper on Irene's desk, and fell panting into his own seat.

The very first period was Social Studies. Miss Arnold called on Irene to make her report. Irene quickly took out the paper. She had been too busy and flustered even to glance at it. She wasn't worried. After all, Minny never made a mistake. The machine was always right. She had no reason to expect that there would be anything wrong with this report. She got up, glanced down at the paper, and began to read:

"The products of Peru. Within the erpivances of herpitaf m-m-m-many erminals p-p-p-ik! Brrr!"

"What?" said Miss Arnold.

Irene automatically kept on reading, while at the same time she felt a kind of dreadful astonishment at herself.

"The wool of gl-gl-gl itsnik nergle t-t-ttrips that can be oh-oh-oh brrr!"

She caught herself then, and stopped. She looked down the rest of the sheet. It was all the same kind of gibberish to the very bottom of the page.

"Irene!" Miss Arnold said. "What on earth—?"

"I'm sorry," Irene said, thinking fast. "I'm— I've got a frog in my throat."

"Sounds like a frog with hiccups," snickered Robin Glenn, who sat in front of her.

Irene pretended to clear her throat. She could remember feeding the information about Peru into the computer. Frowning with the effort to recall the details, she brought to mind the exact pages of the textbook: pages 93, 94, and 95. She pretended to read from the report but really began to recite from memory: "The products of Peru. Within the boundaries of Peru many minerals are to be found, among them silver and copper. . . ."

She went on, digging into her memory until she had covered all she could think of. Then, red-faced, she drew a deep breath and said, "I guess that's all."

"Very good, Irene," said Miss Arnold. "I was a little startled at first, but you've done well. Will you leave your report with me, please."

"Uh—Miss Arnold, it's kind of scribbled," Irene gulped. "And I'd—I'd like to copy it so that I can keep it for my own reference. Can I turn it in tomorrow?"

"All right. Now we come to the geography of Peru. Victoria Williams, please report."

Irene sat down, sighing with relief. Then she glanced over her shoulder. Danny was grinning at her.

She tightened her lips, and gave him a look as sharp and cold as an icicle. Then she turned back to her desk. She was hurt and angry. She knew Danny was full of fun, but she had never expected him to play a trick like this on her.

CHAPTER TWELVE

The Professor Returns

After school, Irene began walking home by herself. Danny came running after her.

"Hey!" he called. "What's the matter?"

She whirled on him. "How can you talk to me, Danny Dunn?" she snapped. "If that's your idea of a joke—"

"Huh?" His mouth dropped open. "A joke? What do you mean?"

"As if you didn't know."

She whipped out the paper and handed it to him. Danny looked at it, and slowly his expression changed; his face grew pale.

"I didn't do this," he whispered.

Irene stared at him. "You mean, it was the machine?"

"Yes. Something's wrong."

"But what could be wrong?"

"I don't know. But—oh, gosh!—we'd better find out right away."

He started to run, and Irene had a little trouble keeping up with him. But she panted bravely along behind him, and at last, winded and wet, they arrived at Danny's front door.

Dan was just reaching for the knob when the door was pulled open.

"Hullo, my boy," cried a well-known, jolly voice.

"Professor Bullfinch!" Danny said.

"Glad to see you, Dan." The Professor's eyes twinkled behind his glasses. He looked well, but tired. "And Irene. How are you?"

"Fine," said Irene, with no enthusiasm.

"You're back sooner than I thought," Danny said, trying to be calm.

"Well, I must say, that's a fine greeting."

"I'm sorry. Of course I'm glad to see you." Danny grinned feebly and shook hands. "Have you—looked at Minny yet?"

The Professor laughed. "Just got in, not ten minutes ago. I'll get to Minny soon enough. I know you'll be just as excited as I am. Look here, here's someone you'll be glad to see."

Danny and Irene came into the living room where two men were sitting. One of them was the Professor's old friend, Dr. A. J. Grimes, a scientist, who was tall and thin and sour-faced. The other was a stranger, a fat man with enormously heavy eyebrows and at least three chins.

101

Danny greeted Dr. Grimes and introduced Irene to him. Then the Professor led him to the stranger, and said, "This is Dr. Ambrose Quibberly, of the Federal Research Council."

"How do you do?" said Danny.

"Dr. Quibberly has come down to inspect Miniac," the Professor went on. "The government has an immediate need for computers of this type, provided Minny turns out to be all we say she is." And he chuckled, and rubbed his hands together.

"Yes, and the sooner we find out, the better," said Dr. Quibberly. "I'm a busy man, you know."

Just then, Mrs. Dunn entered with a large silver tray on which was the Professor's best tea service. She set it down, and began pouring tea.

"Hello, Danny dear," she said. "And Irene! How nice to see you. Run along to the kitchen, Dan, and bring in the plate of cakes I left on the counter."

Danny, with a despairing look at Irene, did as his mother asked.

Mrs. Dunn said, "Now, gentlemen, I know you're all tired from your trip, and I have a pretty good notion of all the work you're going to have to do in the laboratory. So I suggest that instead of rushing into things, you relax and rest. I'll have dinner ready early, and after dinner you can get to work."

"A splendid idea, my dear Mrs. Dunn," the Professor beamed. "And very sensible. Don't you think so, Dr. Quibberly?"

"No," said Dr. Quibberly. "I think—"

Mrs. Dunn put a teacup in his hand. "Lemon or cream?" she asked gently.

"Thank you, neither. I think—"

Danny came back with the plate of cakes and began passing them round. He said nervously to the Professor, "Are you going right in to show them Minny?"

"No, I believe we'll do as your mother has just suggested, and relax. I, for one, am exhausted from the trip down."

"Oh, good," Danny said, and then quickly added, "I mean, I think that's a good idea."

"There's no point in rushing," Dr. Grimes said, gruffly. "The computer probably won't work anyway. Your theories, my dear Bullfinch, are always far beyond any possible practice."

"Not in this case," Professor Bullfinch replied.

"Look here," Dr. Quibberly began, "I haven't got all the time in the world—"

"Certainly not, sir," said Mrs. Dunn soothingly. "Who has? Do have one of these cakes."

"Thank you. Now, I think—"

"Relax, Quibberly," said Dr. Grimes. "You'll pop a blood vessel."

"You won't regret waiting," said the Professor. "Mrs. Dunn's dinners are famous. And it's quite true that we'll work better when we're a little more rested."

He stood up. "Grimes," he said, "it's months since we played a duet. What about a little music?"

"An excellent idea." Dr. Grimes went out into the hall and opened his valise. He took out a small, black case. Meantime, the Professor had taken an enormous bull fiddle from a closet in the living room.

"Do you think this is the time for duets?" Dr. Quibberly fumed. "Really, Professor Bullfinch, I do believe—"

"I agree with you," cried the Professor, heartily. "There's no time like the present, for music. Tune up, Grimes."

Dr. Grimes had taken out a piccolo and was fitting it together. Danny looked at Irene and motioned with his head towards the door. Without a word, the two young people slipped quietly out of the room.

104

"Come on," Danny said, in an urgent whisper, when they were in the hall. "Let's go to the lab."

"Do you think it's safe?"

"Sure. They're good for at least half an hour of music. Then they'll start arguing as they always do and it will break up."

He led the way to the laboratory. Irene remained at the door to warn him if anyone came. Danny went at once to the computer, snapped the POWER ON switch, and fidgeted impatiently until the machine warmed up. Then he began testing all its different parts.

Half an hour later, he shook his head wearily. "I don't know," he said. "If I only had more time, maybe I could—"

"Shh!" Irene hissed. "They're coming."

Danny sprang away from the console. A moment later, the Professor entered, followed by the other two men.

"Right in here, gentlemen," the Professor was saying. "We can at least take a look at Miniac before dinner."

He blinked at Danny. "Why, Dan," he said. "What are you doing?"

"I—I—I was just warming Minny up, Professor," the boy stammered. "I knew you wouldn't want to waste time later."

Danny gulped, but couldn't say anything.

"That's very good of you."

"Do you mean to say," demanded Dr. Quibberly, "that you allow a little child to meddle with your computer? Why, I never heard of such a thing."

"Danny's not a little child," the Professor said, quietly. "He's my assistant. He has lived in this house almost all his life, and he's learned a great deal more than most adults know about science. Of course I trust him."

Danny gulped miserably, but couldn't say anything.

The Professor moved to the console. His foot struck something on the floor. He bent and picked it up; it was a scout knife.

"Is this yours, Dan?" he asked.

"I guess so," Danny said, taking the knife.

"Hm. It's careless to leave tools lying about," said the Professor. "Put it away, my boy."

Danny dropped it into his back pocket.

Dr. Quibberly had stepped forward to examine the console. "Very interesting," he said. "As long as we're here, Bullfinch, perhaps we could begin with a few simple tests."

But just at that instant, Mrs. Dunn looked in round the door. "Everything's hot!" she called. "Come to the table."

Danny blew out a long breath of relief. His fate had been postponed—at least till after dinner.

CHAPTER THIRTEEN

A Dismal Dinner for Danny

They all sat down around the long, oak dining table. Mrs. Dunn had invited Irene to stay for dinner, and when the girl had run across and secured permission from her parents, she returned and sat next to Danny. The two tried to eat, although neither of them had much of an appetite.

But, fortunately, the adults were so busy with their own eating and talking that they hardly noticed the young people.

Dr. Grimes, his vinegary face wrinkled in a smile, said, "Ah, Mrs. Dunn, this roast beef is delicious."

"Thank you. Have some more dumplings, Dr. Grimes. I remembered how much you liked them."

"I must make a point of coming down to visit more often."

"Good!" cried the Professor. "After a month or two of Mrs. Dunn's cooking and my music, you'll be a different man."

109

"Really? Who will he be?" asked Dr. Quibberly, absent-mindedly.

"Oh, he'll still be Dr. Grimes—but a fat and jolly-looking Dr. Grimes," laughed the Professor.

Dr. Quibberly raised his head and peered at Dr. Grimes. "I find it impossible to imagine such a thing," he said.

"Nothing is impossible to imagine," said the Professor. "To a scientist, all things are possible. And the next step is to make them happen."

"Like your computer, eh, Bullfinch?" Dr. Grimes said. "That is, if it really works."

"I think I may confidently say that you will be surprised," said the Professor.

Danny groaned.

"What did you say, Dan?" his mother asked.

"Er—I said—uh—please pass the data."

"The what?"

"I mean, the dumplings."

Dr. Quibberly was saying, "And do you mean that you can really give instructions to your computer by simply speaking to it?"

"Exactly. You know that the large digital computers—like International Business Machines' large computer Number 705, for instance —have push buttons for the memory address se-

lector. However, my machine can receive instructions and addresses by the voice pattern coming through the microphone—"

"And does it reply with a voice?" asked Dr.
Grimes.

"No, no. By means of an electric typewriter.
I have also eliminated punch cards, because of
my new magnetic tape."

"Fantastic."

"Yes, it is. Danny can tell you about it. He's
seen it in operation and has been keeping it up to
date for me while I've been away. Haven't you,
Dan?"

"Eep!" said Danny. He managed a faint
shadow of a smile. "I—I sure have, Professor,"
he got out, at last.

Mrs. Dunn served dessert—fresh, hot peach
pie—and Danny could not manage to eat more
than two pieces. Then he leaned over and whispered something to Irene.

The Professor pulled a number of sheets of
ruled paper from his jacket pocket. "Now, gentlemen," he said, as Mrs. Dunn cleared the table
and brought out the coffee, "before we go in for
the first tests, let us program our material. I have
blanks right here on which we can set down the
necessary operations and addresses."

"Is your programming similar to that used for other computers?"

"In general, yes."

They drew their chairs close together and began to work. An hour went by and then the Professor gathered together the papers.

"I think," he said, "we're ready to begin."

He pushed back his chair and rose. "Danny, my boy," he said, "you may lead the way . . ."

He pulled off his glasses and looked round the dining room.

"Where is the boy?" he asked.

"He has probably run out to play with his little friend," said Dr. Quibberly.

"Hmm. That's strange. I was sure he'd want to see this," said Professor Bullfinch. "Well, we will have to commence without him. Please follow me."

CHAPTER FOURTEEN

Sabotage!

Danny and Irene were not playing. They had slipped out to the laboratory, where Danny once again tried to find out what was wrong with the computer. He examined the social studies report carefully in the hope of finding a clue, and once more checked over all the parts of the machine. He stood up, at last, wiping his forehead, and said, "I give up."

"Perhaps we'd better just tell the Professor."

Danny drew a deep breath. "Gosh!" he said. "I don't know how to."

"Just *tell* him."

"Sure. It's not so easy. You know how grown-ups are when you try to explain anything."

"Even the Professor?"

"No . . . but he trusted me, and this is such an important thing, and—" Danny looked helplessly at the console. "I've tried everything I can think of. If only I could get some kind of hint. How could it have happened? What went wrong?"

"Well, you'll have to make up your mind right now whether to tell him or not," Irene said. "Because I hear them coming."

Almost as she spoke, the three men entered the laboratory.

"Ah," said the Professor. "Here you are, Dan. I knew you wouldn't miss this. All warmed up?"

"Yes, Professor," Danny said, wretchedly. Then he straightened up, and said, "I want to—"

But the Professor was not listening. He and his two companions grouped themselves purposefully at the console, and spread out their papers.

Dr. Grimes said, "Now for this first test, we have already worked out the course of a rocket traveling at 9273 miles per hour. It only remains to check the procedures and steps on your computer."

"And we'll want a time check, also," said Dr. Quibberly.

"Listen, I want to—" Danny began again.

Dr. Quibberly turned and frowned at him. "Shh!" he said.

The Professor had already cleared the machine's memory and had tapped the key marked INSTRUCTIONS. He was reading a set of figures into the microphone, while Dr. Grimes made notations.

Danny cleared his throat. Once again, Dr.

His usually jovial face took on a serious look.

Quibberly gazed at him, his enormous eyebrows waggling angrily. Danny shrugged helplessly and was silent.

The computer hummed and clucked, and the tiny lights twinkled, marking the location in its memory of each step of its instructions. Then the typewriter began to chatter.

"Aha!" cried the Professor. "How was that? Only ninety-three seconds."

"Not bad," Dr. Quibberly said. "Let's look at the results."

The Professor, with a broad smile, pulled the paper from the typewriter.

"Here we are," he said. "Ah . . . oh-oh-oh-ikk! Mgrf sizippl b-b-b-brr!"

"What?" cried Dr. Grimes.

The smile faded from the Professor's face. Hastily, he took off his glasses and wiped them. Then he picked up the paper again. "Oogl blerp," he read.

"I beg your pardon?" said Dr. Quibberly. "Blerp?"

"Dear me," said the Professor. "I don't understand. Something must have happened to. . . ." His voice died away, and slowly he turned. His usually jovial face took on a serious look.

"Danny!" he said.

Danny sighed. "I tried to tell you, Professor," he said. "Honest, I wanted to. But you were in such a hurry, and I was sort of scared, and anyway I'm sure it wasn't anything I did, and anyway . . ."

"Ha!" Dr. Quibberly exclaimed. "Very interesting. Very interesting indeed. You allow this little boy to play with your computer as if it were a—a game of marbles. You needn't be surprised if it can only produce noises like *blerp*."

Dr. Grimes was looking very sour. "On the other hand," he said, "it is possible that the computer wasn't very good to begin with. I must say, Bullfinch, there have been times when your theories have run away with you, and perhaps this is one of them."

"One moment," said the Professor. He never lost his air of calm. He took out his pipe and began to fill it slowly, and in a mild voice said, "All right, Dan. Suppose you tell me just what did happen."

"Well," Danny said, "to begin with, we used it to help us do our homework."

The mouths of the two visitors opened wide, and even the Professor looked shaken at this.

Danny went on and told the whole story: how

he had come to think of using the computer as a homework machine, how Miss Arnold had objected, and how he had quickly run off Irene's social studies report which had appeared as gibberish. When he had finished, even Dr. Quibberly was looking at him with a certain amount of respect, while Dr. Grimes was almost grinning and the Professor was frankly chuckling with amusement.

"I see," Professor Bullfinch said. "It's quite a tale, my boy. I don't think we need go into all the details of it right now. There are a couple of points I think I ought to discuss with you later, such as the matter of counting up to a million by thousands—"

"Yes, sir," Danny said meekly.

"Hmm! Well, never mind that now. I believe the matter is fairly simple, gentlemen. It won't take long to fix."

"Very well," said Dr. Grimes.

"But be quick about it," Dr. Quibberly said, glancing at a big, old-fashioned silver pocket watch. "We've waited long enough already."

The Professor rolled up his sleeves and went to work. The minutes ticked by, with Dr. Quibberly growing more and more impatient and Dr. Grimes looking grimmer and grimmer. Finally, the Professor straightened up. His round face was flushed, and his bald head shining with perspiration.

"I'm afraid I can't locate the trouble," he said. "I felt sure it was in the output, or the translating mechanism which operates the typewriter—"

"Perhaps it's those new switches of yours," Dr. Grimes suggested. "It may be that they don't work quite as well as you thought they did. Or perhaps the temperature isn't right."

"I thought of that," said Professor Bullfinch. "But the gauges show that they're operating. And the thermostat is set properly. It's impossible for anything to be wrong there."

Danny gazed at the Professor as if he were about to say something, but then his attention was caught by Dr. Quibberly, who had snapped the case of his watch shut with a decisive click. He put the watch into his vest pocket and buttoned up his jacket.

"I'm sorry," Dr. Quibberly said, "but I feel that we've spent quite enough time on this—this miserable demonstration of ineptitude."

"Really, Dr. Quibberly," said the Professor, "if you can only wait a little longer—"

"I'm sorry. I can't wait for foolishness."

Irene, standing next to Danny, looked at her

friend with astonishment. "What's the matter? Are you cold?" she asked.

Danny's teeth were chattering and his knees shaking.

"C-c-cold with nervousness," he muttered. "We can't get him lo. I m-m-mean, we c-c-can't let him go!"

"You sound just like I did when I started to read my report."

Danny could not help grinning, but it was a weak and sickly grin.

The Professor said, "I'm sure I can repair the computer. I can't imagine what caused the trouble, but I know—"

Dr. Grimes snorted. "Maybe it's sabotage, Bullfinch," he said jeeringly.

"Good-by, gentlemen," said Dr. Quibberly. He started for the door.

A cold sweat broke out on Danny's forehead. He reached into his pocket and pulled out his handkerchief, to wipe his face. There was a loud clatter as two objects fell on the floor. The noise stopped Dr. Quibberly.

Danny looked down. On the floor were two identical boy scout knives.

He grabbed them up. He was red with embarrassment. Something crumbled between his fingers, and he gaped at the knives for a moment; then he raised his eyes to stare first at the Professor, then Dr. Grimes, then at Irene.

Then he shouted, "Sabotage! Cold! Of course—that's it!"

CHAPTER FIFTEEN

The Chilly Computer

For an instant there was a stunned silence. Then Dr. Quibberly said, "The boy's hysterical."

"Take it easy, Dan," the Professor said. He went to Danny and took him by the arms. "Control yourself. It really isn't that important."

"Listen—I'm serious," Danny cried. "I can prove it. I know what's wrong."

"Get him some castor oil," Dr. Grimes commanded. "Or an aspirin."

"Wait a minute," said the Professor. "Go on, Danny. What is it?"

"Well, first of all, when you found that scout knife on the floor a while ago and gave it to me, I thought it was mine because it looks just like mine. But here's mine. This one belongs to Sni—to Eddie Philips."

"Eddie Philips?"

"An international spy, no doubt," Dr. Grimes said.

"No. A boy in my class. He's the one who

sneaked up here and watched us using the machine, and then told Miss Arnold."

"How do you know it's his knife?" Irene asked. "I mean, if they both look alike—"

"Why, you ought to know, too," Danny said. "Look at it. The handle's got dried mud all over it."

"Oh!" Irene giggled. "Mud! Of course."

"He must have forgotten the knife when he came here to wreck the machine. I knew he'd try to get even, and that's what he did. The machine is *cold*."

"Cold? I don't understand," said the Professor. "The power is on."

"Sure it is. It's your switches that are cold."

"But the thermostat is set for the proper temperature. Look it it—98.6°."

"That's right. But I'll bet if we take the cover of the thermostat off, we'll find that the dial is disconnected from the refrigerator control."

Danny opened the screw driver blade of the scout knife and unscrewed the cover of the thermostat. Inside, the indicator dial had been connected to the temperature control lever by means of a small bolt. Danny pointed. The bolt had been removed. No matter where the dial was

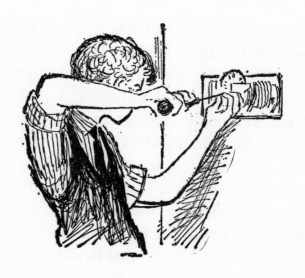

set, the control still remained at its coldest point.

"The temperature inside the case must be about ten below zero," Danny said. "You see, Eddie was watching us when I explained about your new switches to Irene and Joe. He heard what I said about never touching the thermostat. He knows something about machinery—he's really not stupid. So he must have slipped into the lab after we left, and using the screw driver blade of his knife, as I just did, he opened the thermostat and took out the bolt. He set the control as far down as it would go and put the cover back. Then, when I came in to lock up, he ducked out the window but forgot his knife."

"How did you ever suspect it?" Irene said.

"Why, when you asked me if I was cold and said that I sounded just like your report, I began to wonder if that could be it," Danny replied. He grinned at the Professor. "And when *you* said that because the thermostat was set at the right temperature it was *impossible* for anything to be wrong—well, I remembered that time when I started to turn off the power because I thought there was something wrong with the machine. You told me then that a scientist should never take anything for granted. Remember?"

The Professor bit his lips. Then, rubbing the top of his head, he chuckled ruefully. "Yes, I do remember it," he said. "My dear boy, you've taught me my own lesson. I'll try to keep it in mind, in the future."

"Do you mean to say," asked Dr. Grimes, "that that's the only thing wrong with the computer?"

Danny nodded. Briskly, he replaced the bolt so that the indicator dial was connected once more with the temperature control lever. He set the dial at the proper temperature.

"You should have a thermometer on the outside of the case, Bullfinch, to show the inside temperature," said Dr. Grimes. "You see, I told you you were impractical."

"Well, it's difficult to think of everything," said the Professor. "I believe enough time has passed, gentlemen. Let's try once more."

Dr. Quibberly had returned to the console, and the three men bent over the machine once again. The Professor fed in the data and instructions and then pressed the operating key.

"Ninety-one seconds, this time," he said. "There you are."

He pulled the paper from the typewriter.

"Exactly right," said Dr. Grimes, examining the answer.

They ran three more complicated tests. And each time Miniac was correct to the last decimal point.

Dr. Quibberly blew out his lips. "It appears," he said, "that I must apologize to you—and to this young man as well. I must say, I was wrong when I called him a little child. I would venture to predict that he will some day be a credit to the world of science."

"Yes," said Dr. Grimes, "if he can keep out of trouble long enough to get through school."

"Nonsense, Grimes," said the Professor.

"How can anyone be a scientist without stirring things up, asking questions, jumping into things headlong with both feet?"

Irene snickered. "It's kind of hard, Professor, to jump headlong with both feet."

The Professor turned red, as they all laughed.

"Well," he said, "you know what I mean. Anyway, remember that for a scientist, nothing is impossible."

Danny whispered something to Irene. She nodded. He said, "Professor—speaking of school, can I ask for one favor?"

"Certainly, my boy. What is it?"

"Can we keep on using Minny for our homework?"

"Hmm." The Professor turned to Dr. Quibberly. "Do you think, now, that the government will be interested in Miniac?"

"I certainly do."

"Well, I should imagine that we'll have a few weeks before we have to send it to Washington," said the Professor. "Suppose we say three weeks more, Danny."

"Fine!" said Danny. "That'll just take us to the end of the term, without having to do any more homework."

The Professor rubbed his chin and smiled. "That's right," he said. "But at the same time, my boy, remember what you just taught me—don't take anything for granted!"

CHAPTER SIXTEEN

Snitcher Gets a Present

It was the last day of school. The pupils were gathered in groups about the classroom, comparing their marks and report cards. The room was full of excited chatter and laughter; fortunately, no one had failed to pass.

Eddie Philips was standing in a corner with George Bessel and one or two of his other friends, boasting about how well he had done in the final exams.

"It was a snap," he said. "I knew I was going to get an A."

"What do you think that A stands for?" giggled Ellen Tresselt, who was standing nearby. "All wet?"

"Oh, dear, no," said Robin Glenn. "It stands for *A* big bag of wind."

Eddie scowled. Before he could retort, however, Danny pushed his way past the girls and confronted him.

"Oh, Eddie," Danny said, innocently, "I've been trying to see you all day."

"Yeah? What for?" Eddie asked, suspiciously.

"I found this knife, and somebody said it looked like yours."

Eddie examined the scout knife Dan held out on the palm of his hand.

"It's mine," he said.

"Are you sure? Can you prove it?"

"Sure I'm sure. I can tell by that place where the stag handle is nicked. And the ring is bent, too."

Danny slowly opened the big blade of the knife. "Gee, I'm glad of that," he said. "I wouldn't want there to be any mistake about whose knife this is. You see, there's something on the blade."

He held out the knife. The others crowded round, and began laughing. On the blade, using a power tool, Danny had engraved the word SNITCHER.

Eddie turned crimson. Danny snapped the blade shut and tossed the knife to him.

"Next time, Snitcher, don't leave your things around the Professor's laboratory," Danny said. "It's so messy."

For once, Eddie had nothing to say.

Danny left him and walked back to the blackboard where Irene had been standing, watching the whole scene.

"That ought to take care of him for a while," Danny chuckled.

131

"Yes, Danny, and I told you it would be more effective than just punching him in the nose," Irene replied.

"You were right." Danny looked at her, and sighed deeply. "Gee, Irene," he said, "you're a swell girl."

"That's true," said a voice behind him, "but you don't have to get all mushy about it."

It was Joe. He was trying not to smile, and blushing at the same time. He said, "I think it's about time we made up, Irene. I'm sorry for the things I said a few weeks ago."

"Oh, Joe, I forgot all about that day," Irene said. "Why, we've been working together for the last three weeks and you haven't said a single thing about girls being nothing but trouble."

"Yeah. Well, I'm glad we had the homework machine. And I guess I was wrong all around. Look at my report card. This is the first time I ever got an A in arithmetic."

"I'm glad, Joe."

"So'm I. And—and I—well, I have something for you."

Irene and Danny looked at him in surprise.

"It's not much," Joe mumbled. "Just a poem. Here—"

He thrust a piece of paper into Irene's hand. She opened it, and read:

Who is the one who made me change my mind about girls being not so keen?

Irene.

What do I think of when I am looking out of a train window and get tired of the scene?

Irene.

If I were Jack Sprat and could eat no fat, who would I want to eat no lean?

Irene.

Who will I pin up if I have to go into the army when I am eighteen?

Irene.

Whose eyes are as blue as a new pair of jeans?

Irene's.

If I were a jar of yellow paint, and she were a jar of blue, with who would I want to mix, to make green?

Irene.

"Why, Joe," Irene exclaimed. "It's beautiful!"

Danny stuck out his lower lip. He had been reading over Irene's shoulder. "Pooh!" he said. "He keeps saying 'who' instead of 'whom.' He sure didn't pay any attention when we fed the grammar books into the computer."

"Oh, Danny," said Irene. "I believe you're jealous."

"Me?" Danny said indignantly. Then he grinned. "Yep," he said. "I am."

Miss Arnold came towards them, just then, and put a hand on Danny's shoulder. "Well,

133

my three star pupils," she said. "Congratulations. I know your marks are the highest in the class."

"Thanks, Miss Arnold," they all said.

Miss Arnold's eyes twinkled. "Now that the term is over," she went on, "I have something important to tell you. It's about your homework."

"Our—our homework?" Danny said uneasily.

Joe groaned. "It seems to me we went through this before."

Miss Arnold nodded. "Yes, your homework. I'd like you three to wait until the other pupils have gone. I'll only keep you a few minutes. Please come to my desk when the room is empty. . . ."

CHAPTER SEVENTEEN

The Homework Champions

Professor Bullfinch and Dr. Grimes were playing a duet in the living room, when Danny came home from school. He came in slowly, scuffling his feet, his head hanging, and a gloomy expression on his face.

He tossed his books on the bench in the hall. His mother came downstairs with her shopping basket over her arm. She kissed him, and then held him off and looked him up and down.

"Why, Danny dear," she said, "whatever is the matter?"

"Nothing."

"Didn't you do well in the exams? You passed, didn't you?"

Silently, he handed her his report card.

The Professor leaned his bullfiddle against a chair and came to see the card. "Top marks," he said. "Then why so growlsome looking? Are you unhappy because school is over?"

"What?" said Danny. "Do you think I'm crazy?"

135

Mrs. Dunn folded her arms. "Daniel Dunn," she said, in her no-nonsense voice. "Out with it! Something's wrong."

Danny kicked at the rug with one toe. "Oh . . . well you know how hard we worked on the computer so we wouldn't have to do any homework?"

"Yes?"

"Well, Miss Arnold just broke the news to us that we've been doing homework all along. In fact—we got special honors for doing more and harder homework than any of the other kids in class!"

Mrs. Dunn began to bubble with mirth. Dr. Grimes came out, raising his eyebrows.

Professor Bullfinch coughed, and said, "I wondered how long it would be before you found that out. Naturally, in order to feed information into the computer you had to know it yourselves. And in order to give the machine the proper instructions for solving problems, you had to know how to solve them yourselves. So, of course, you had to do homework—and plenty of it."

"Why, simply programming a problem is homework," Dr. Grimes put in.

"Yes. It just never occurred to me before," Danny confessed. "Gosh, it—it somehow doesn't seem fair."

"It wasn't really fair for you to expect a machine to do all your work for you, was it?" Mrs. Dunn said, gently. "That's why I suggested to Miss Arnold that she give you high school homework to do."

"You suggested it? My own mother! But why?"

"Surely that must be obvious to you, Danny. I knew you'd have to study quite hard to keep up with it. And after all, darling, that's what homework is for—to teach you how to study by yourself."

Danny sighed. "I guess so. Well, nobody can complain that we haven't studied this year."

"And you've done more than that," said the Professor, enthusiastically. "Come into the living room and listen to what Grimes and I have been doing."

He and Dr. Grimes returned to their instruments. They sat down before some sheets of music and, after a little tuning up, began to play. Danny and his mother listened thoughtfully. It was a rather dull piece of music.

137

When it was over, Danny said, "Well, it wasn't too bad. Who wrote it?"

"Minny did," answered the Professor.

"Minny?"

"Certainly. We got the idea for the experiment from something Joe said, a long time ago—he asked what would happen if we sang into the microphone. And you youngsters apparently got Miniac to write your school reports for you—"

"So you got the machine to write music?"

"Yes. We fed into it full instructions for the composition of a sonata, plus information on note relationships and a lot of other technical material. Then we programmed a sonata for piccolo and bullfiddle, and Miniac turned it out. We had to add an attachment for writing music notes, of course. . . ."

Mrs. Dunn laughed. "It isn't bad," she said, "but it isn't exactly Beethoven, either."

Professor Bullfinch shook his head. "No. It never can be Beethoven, Mrs. Dunn. No matter how intelligent the computer is, it is only a machine. It can solve problems in minutes that would take a man months to work out. But behind it there must be a human brain. It can

never be a creator of music or of stories, or paint-
ings, or ideas. It cannot even do our homework
for us—*we* must do the homework. The machine can only help, as a textbook helps. It can
only be a tool, as a typewriter is a tool."

"I said that, didn't I?" Danny asked.

"Yes, dear," his mother replied. "You said it.
But I don't think you really thought about it—
until now."

Joe stuck his head in the front door. "Hello,
Mrs. Dunn," he said. "Is Danny around? Oh,

hi, Dan. Come on out. Irene and I are going down to the drug store to celebrate with a soda."

"Fine," said Mrs. Dunn. "Run along, Dan. And—" She slipped an arm about his shoulders and hugged him tight. "I don't care whether it's fair or not, but I'm very proud of you."

Danny suddenly felt a lot better.

"Thanks, Mom," he said, hugging her in return. Then he went to join his friends.

The three walked down the shady street together, Irene between the two boys. She said, "First prize for homework. How do you like that?"

"It's the end of using this computer for homework," Danny said. "Never again! I don't even want to think about machines."

Joe thrust his hands deep into his pockets. "You can't beat the system," he grumbled. "Teachers are too smart for kids. That's all there is to it. Now if only—"

Irene caught hold of his arm. "Look," she said. "Look at Danny."

Danny had a strange, wild look in his eyes, and a faraway smile on his lips.

"Oh-oh. Here we go again," said Joe.

Irene said, "Danny—count up to a billion by thousands—quick!"

"Oh, don't be silly," Danny said. "This is just a simple idea I had. Listen—what about a *teaching* machine . . . ?

"Grab his other arm, Joe," Irene shouted. "He needs a soda—fast."

They seized his arms and ran, dragging him along, to the drug store.

JAY WILLIAMS is best known for his adult historical novels, among them *Solomon and Sheba* and *The Witches*. He has written six works of nonfiction also, and ten juveniles in addition to the Danny Dunn books he has written with Raymond Abrashkin. His work has appeared in many anthologies and text books. Born in Buffalo, New York, Mr. Williams was educated at the University of Pennsylvania, Columbia University, and the Art Students' League. He saw service during World War II with the 65th Infantry Division from 1943 to 1945 and received the Purple Heart. In 1949 he was awarded a Guggenheim Fellowship.

RAYMOND ABRASHKIN is the author and co-producer of the very popular and successful film *Little Fugitive*. He has done a Picture News Series called "Life with Junior," with a group of experts including Dr. Benjamin Spock; and also, for *The Ladies' Home Journal*, a series called "Bringing Up Parents," with Dr. Barbara Biber of the Bank Street College, New York City. In addition to over fifty children's records, he has written the librettos for four children's operas. Born in Brooklyn in 1911, Mr. Abrashkin received his B.S. degree from City College of New York and taught in the New York public schools. Following service in the U.S. Maritime Service he was an editor at Reynal and Hitchcock, and since 1946 has devoted his full time to free-lance work.

EZRA JACK KEATS, Caldecott-Award winner for *The Snowy Day,* has illustrated many children's books, including Jay Williams' and Raymond Abrashkin's Danny Dunn stories. He was born and raised in Brooklyn, and after high school there attended the Art Student League in Manhattan. Later he taught illustrating at the Famous Artists' School in Westport, Connecticut. Besides spending a year in Paris, his on-the-spot research for book illustrations has taken him to many different locations, including Cuba and Scotland. Mr. Keats now lives in New York City.